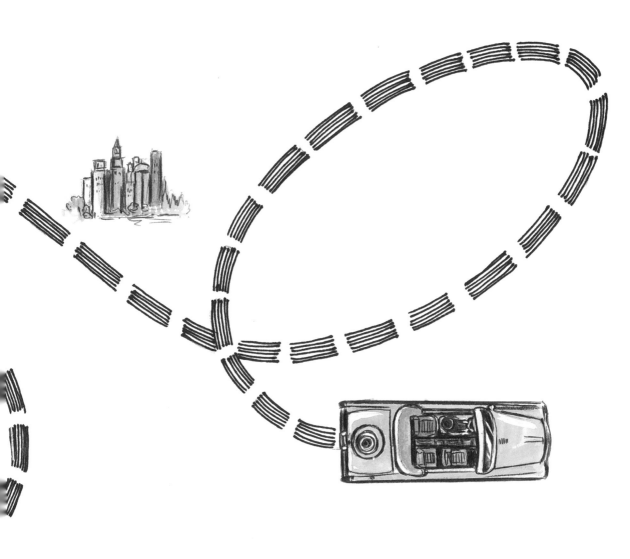

This Book Belongs To:

Willie the TAXI Cat

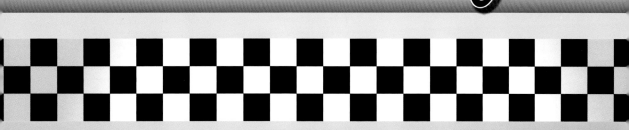

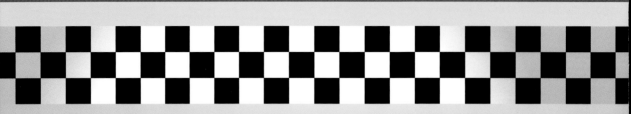

Written and Illustrated by
Eva M. Sakmar-Sullivan

4880 Lower Valley Road • Atglen, PA 19310

Willie, the Taxi Cat, drives creatures everywhere!

cool critters and carousing

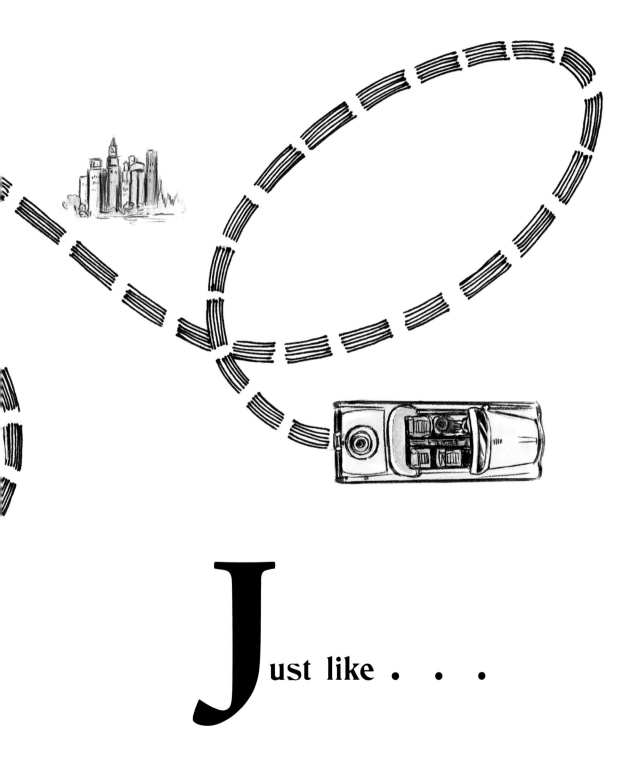

J ust like . . . .

O

ne wildly whiskered

whistling weasel

1

T

wo toe-tapping, tuba-toting

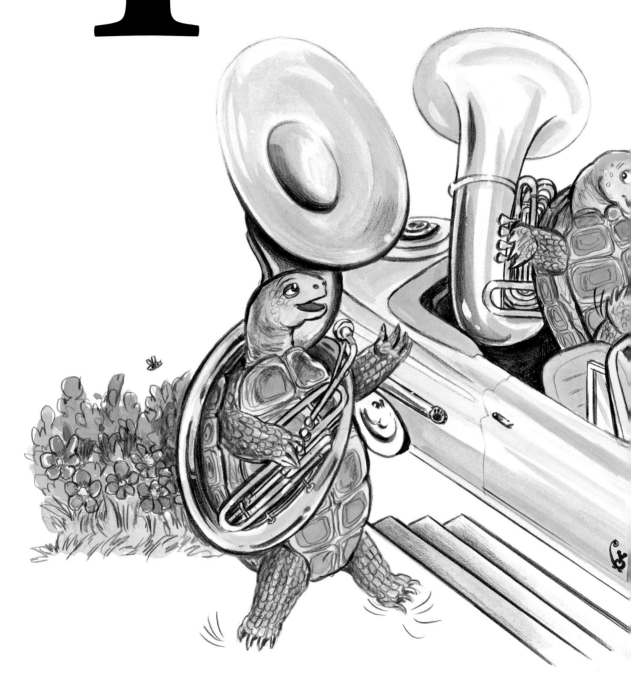

urtles.

2

T

hree terrifically tressed

...antalizing tigers.

3

F

our fiddling, fabulously

fitted, fanciful frogs.

4

F

ive flirtatiously frocked

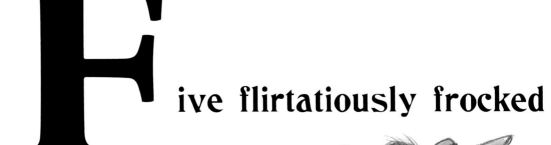

fun-loving foxes.

5

S

ix sassy, but sweet

soda-sipping swans.

6

S

even sumptuously striped,

speed-skating, scholarly skunks.

7

E

ight extremely agile,

elegantly attired elephants.

8

N

ine noisy,
newts.

naughty-but-nice, near-sighted

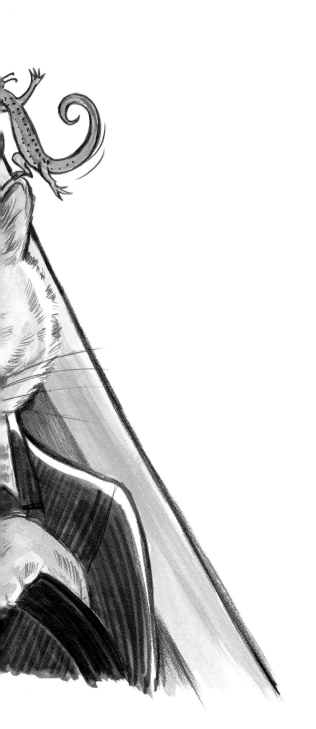

9

Ten tumbling, totally tremendous, tuxedoed turkeys

10

Dedication

To Willie, an incredible little cat that taught me so much and lived to the remarkable age of 27.

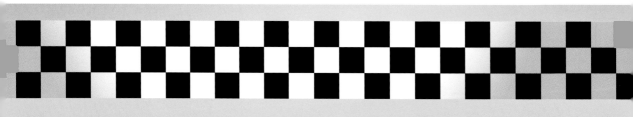

I would also like to fondly remember Willie's "partners in mischief," Alvin and Spider. Much gratitude and appreciation to the "regal" Queenie for her feline patience while posing for all the illustrations of Willie.

About the
Author / Illustrator

Eva M. Sakmar-Sullivan is an author/illustrator whose main goal is to entertain and bring joy to children. She would also like to offer a fun-filled but educational sharing experience between parents or caregivers and their children.

In addition to Eva's love of writing and illustrating children's books, she is also an accomplished visionary artist. Her art invites the viewer to journey to mythic and angelic realms. She is the author of *The Celebration of Love Oracle* and the children's book, *The Silly Looking Thing*.

Enjoy her work at ***www.stardolphin.com***.

The Silly Looking Thing.
Eva M. Sakmar-Sullivan.
Itsy-Bitsy boy frog discovers
that just because someone
looks a little different than
you, doesn't mean you can't
be friends – or at least give
the friendship a chance.
You just might be surprised
or shocked at what you
find out! Little frog was!
Picture book - Ages 0 - 6.

Size: 7" x 10"   33 color illustrations   40pp.
ISBN: 978-0-7643-4144-1   hard cover $16.99

Images and text by Eva M. Sakmar-Sullivan

Copyright © 2013 by Eva M. Sakmar-Sullivan
Library of Congress Control Number: 2012952904

Designed by Mark David Bowyer
Type set in Beaumarchais / Benguiat Bk BT

ISBN: 978-0-7643-4436-7
Printed in China

Schiffer Books are available at special discounts for bulk purchases for sales promotions or premiums. Special editions, including personalized covers, corporate imprints, and excerpts can be created in large quantities for special needs. For more information contact the publisher:

Published by Schiffer Publishing, Ltd.
4880 Lower Valley Road
Atglen, PA 19310
Phone: (610) 593-1777; Fax: (610) 593-2002
E-mail: Info@schifferbooks.com

For the largest selection of fine reference books on this and related subjects, please visit our website at
www.schifferbooks.com
We are always looking for people to write books on new and related subjects. If you have an idea for a book, please contact us at
proposals@schifferbooks.com

This book may be purchased from the publisher.
Please try your bookstore first.
You may write for a free catalog.

In Europe, Schiffer books are distributed by
Bushwood Books
6 Marksbury Ave.
Kew Gardens
Surrey TW9 4JF England
Phone: 44 (0) 20 8392 8585; Fax: 44 (0) 20 8392 9876
E-mail: info@bushwoodbooks.co.uk
Website: www.bushwoodbooks.co.uk

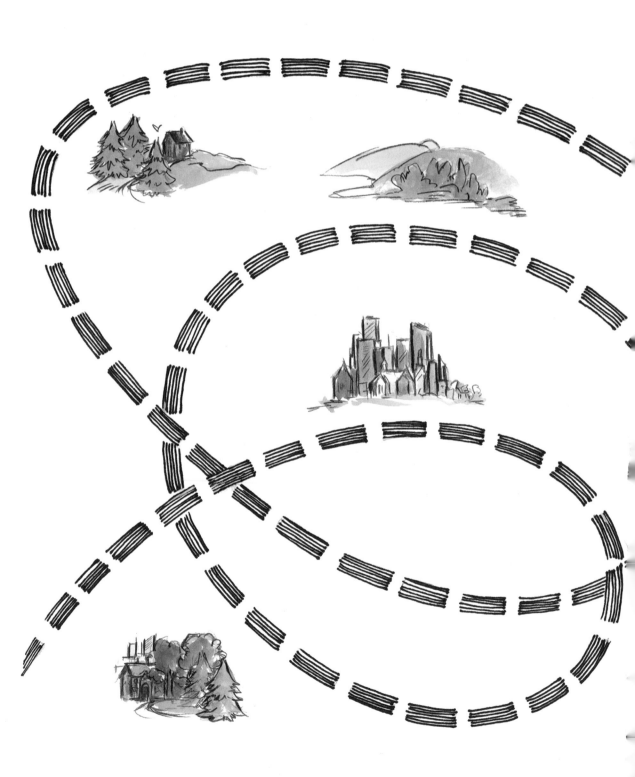